Princess PULVERIZER

GRiLLed cHeese anD DraGons

PENGUIN WORKSHOP
Penguin Young Readers Group
An Imprint of Penguin Random House LLC

Library of Congress Cataloging-in-Publication Data is available.

ISBN 9780515158311 (pbk)   10 9 8 7 6 5 4 3 2 1
ISBN 9780515158328 (hc)   10 9 8 7 6 5 4 3 2 1

CHAPTER 1

"Princess Serena!" Lady Frump shouted angrily. "Come down from there right now! Princesses do not hang from the ceiling."

But the Royal Princess of Empiria was not ready to come down. She didn't want to sit at the table with her classmates, learning about the proper manners to use at a tea party. Who cared how you held your pinkie when you picked up your teacup? Tea parties were no fun at all.

But swinging from the rafters—now, *that* was fun!

The princess began swaying back and forth over the heads of the other girls in her class.

Back and forth.

Back and forth.

Back and forth.

She swung her legs higher and higher in the air.

"Wheeee!" the princess shouted down to her classmates. "You guys should really try this. It's amazing. I feel like I'm flying."

The girls stared up at her in surprise. No one disobeyed Lady Frump. *Ever.* She was the toughest, scariest teacher at the Royal School of Ladylike Manners.

But Lady Frump didn't frighten the princess at all. *Nobody* frightened her.

She was the bravest girl in all of Empiria.

Maybe even in the whole world.

So she just kept swinging.

Back and forth.

Back and . . .

"WHOA!" The princess let out a loud yelp as she lost her grip on the rafters.

SPLASH! The princess's royal bottom landed right in a big bowl of ooey-gooey purplish pomegranate pudding.

SMASH. Spoons, forks, knives, teacups, and saucers crashed to the floor. There was broken china everywhere.

The princess looked up at Lady Frump. The teacher's face was beet red. Her eyes were tightened into tiny angry slits. And she was clutching her handkerchief in a sweaty fist.

"Oops," the princess said sheepishly.

"Now look what you've done!" Lady Frump scolded. "Why didn't you come down carefully when I asked you to, Princess Serena?"

"Well, for one thing, that's not my name," the princess replied. "I've told you that a million times."

A few of the girls gasped.

"Serena is the name your father, King Alexander, gave you," Lady Frump reminded her.

"But it's not the *right* name for me," the princess explained. "Serena comes from the word *serene*. And *serene* means calm and peaceful. I'm neither of those."

Lady Frump couldn't argue with that. *Nobody* could argue with that.

"That's why I gave myself a new name," the princess continued. "From now on, I want everyone to call me Princess Pulverizer."

"Princess Pulverizer is not a proper name for a royal girl," Lady Frump told her.

"Says who?" Princess Pulverizer argued.

"I . . . I . . . well . . . ," Lady Frump stammered.

The girls all stared at Princess Pulverizer in awe. She'd stumped Lady Frump. *Amazing.*

"Never mind," Lady Frump said, wiping her forehead with her handkerchief. "I will have two of the scullions from the kitchen come and clean up this mess later. And you, Princess *Serena*, will help them."

Princess Pulverizer gasped with surprise. She wasn't sure which was more shocking—the idea that her teacher would expect her to clean up the mess with the kitchen maids, or that she refused to call her by her new name.

"In the meantime, we will head into the ballroom to practice dancing the saltarello," Lady Frump continued. "I want all of you to be able to dance beautifully at the ball next month."

Princess Pulverizer frowned as she followed her classmates into the ballroom. The only thing worse than tea-party lessons was dance lessons.

Princess Pulverizer was not a great dancer.

She wasn't even a good dancer.

Actually, she was a *lousy* dancer.

To make matters worse, the ballroom was right above the courtyard where the boys in Knight School did their training. The boys looked like they were having so much fun, riding on their horses and having sword fights. And here she was, stuck moving her feet to the same beat, over and over again.

"Tap, tap, hop. Tap, tap, hop . . . ," Lady Frump repeated as she clapped her hands. "Ladies, please dance to the rhythm."

Princess Pulverizer looked out the window and watched as two of the knights-in-training drew swords. They began fencing, poking each other's armor with their weapons.

Clang. Clang. Every time one of the swords hit their metal suits, it made a loud noise that echoed all the way up to the ballroom.

Clip-clop. Clip-clop. Three other boys rode by on horseback. All of them—even the horses—were dressed in armor.

Princess Pulverizer scowled. It just wasn't fair.

Why did the boys get to wear full suits of armor and ride on horses, while she was stuck trying to hop around a dance floor in a silly lace gown?

And why did the boys get to wear those

valiant visors when they fenced, while she was stuck having to balance a tiara on her head as she danced the saltarello? A visor had a purpose—it kept a knight safe. But what was the point of a tiara?

"Tap, tap, hop . . . Tap, tap, hop . . . ," Lady Frump continued. "Girls! Please pay attention. Tap, tap . . ."

Princess Pulverizer tap-tap-hopped her way over to the window for a better look at the two boys who were fencing. One of them was actually pretty good. He moved his feet quickly and was able to block most of the jabs that came from his opponent.

From Princess Pulverizer's point of view, fencing didn't look that hard. All you had to do was dance around a little and poke at someone with a sword.

A few lunges here.

A few steps backward there.

A poke.

A jab.

And maybe a little twirl—just to make
it look fancy.

What was the big deal about fencing,
anyway?

Lunge.

Step.

Poke.

Jab.

Twirl.

OOMF!

"Whoa!" Princess Pulverizer exclaimed as she bashed into one of the girls in her class.

Who crashed into the girl on her left.

Who knocked down the two girls on either side of her.

Who both collapsed *right on top of Lady Frump.*

"PRINCESS SERENA!" Lady Frump shouted angrily as she climbed out from under the pile of crowns, shoes, petticoats, arms, and legs. "What am I going to do with you?"

Princess Pulverizer looked down at the purplish pudding stain on her dress.

She stared at the wiggling mountain of classmates on the ground.

And for once, the princess had no answer for Lady Frump.

CHAPTER 2

"I can't believe you've been sent home again," King Alexander of Empiria scolded his daughter later that afternoon. "Why can't you behave in school?"

"Because school is boring," Princess Pulverizer told him. "Everything we study is useless! Why do I need to know how to curtsy? Or learn which fork is the right one to use? Or practice staying on the beat when dancing the saltarello?"

"Because those are the things every princess needs to learn," King Alexander explained. "How else will you know how to behave correctly at a banquet, or dance at a ball with grace and elegance?"

"But I don't *want* to be a princess," Princess Pulverizer insisted. "And I don't want to go to banquets or balls. I want to rescue damsels in distress and slay dragons. I want to have sword fights. *I want to be a knight.*"

"Excuse me?" the king asked, surprised.

"A knight," Princess Pulverizer repeated. "I want to go out into the world, have adventures, and earn my place among the Knights of the Skround Table."

Princess Pulverizer looked longingly across the room. The Skround Table was so beautiful—perfectly square, but with carefully rounded corners. *Skround*.

The Skround Table was where the knights gathered to talk about their exciting quests. Princess Pulverizer wanted nothing more than to sit there among them.

To be *one* of them.

"I don't need to go to the Royal School of Ladylike Manners to be a knight," Princess Pulverizer continued. "I need to go to Knight School."

"Actually, knights need to know a lot of the same things you are learning in school," the king told her.

"Like what?" Princess Pulverizer asked.

"Well, you are learning to dance gracefully," the king replied. "Every sword fight is like a dance. A knight who is light on his feet will always win. But a clumsy knight will land on his behind every time."

Princess Pulverizer frowned. It was hard to argue with logic like that. Although . . .

"Does a knight really need to know which fork to use to eat salad?" she asked her father. "Or how to pour a perfect cup of tea?"

The king stared at his daughter. "You've got me there," he admitted.

Princess Pulverizer smiled triumphantly.

"But there are still a lot of other things you can learn from Lady Frump," the king continued. "You need to go back to the Royal School of Ladylike Manners."

Princess Pulverizer's eyes flew open wide in surprise. She couldn't believe her father was making her go back to that horrible place.

"B-b-but you *have* to let me go to

Knight School," Princess Pulverizer insisted.

"Why?" her father asked her.

"Because I *want* to go," Princess Pulverizer told him. "And I'm a princess. Princesses always get what they want."

"Not this time." The king shook his head.

"I *am* going to Knight School," the princess declared. She folded her arms tightly across her chest.

"No, you're not," the king replied. He folded *his* arms tightly across *his* chest. "You are going back to Lady Frump."

"Am not! Am not!

Am not!" Princess Pulverizer started jumping up and down and shouting. "I shouldn't have to listen to Lady Frump. She should have to listen to *me*. *I'm* the princess."

"But she is your teacher," the king said. "In school, *she* is in charge."

Princess Pulverizer shook her head. "This isn't fair!" she shouted. "You won't let me go to Knight School because I'm a girl. That's not right!"

"This has nothing to do with you being a girl," King Alexander told her.

Princess Pulverizer stopped shouting. She stopped jumping up and down. "It doesn't?" she asked.

The king shook his head. "No. It has to do with the fact that you don't have what it takes to be a knight."

"Yes, I do," Princess Pulverizer insisted. "I already know how to ride a horse. And fencing doesn't seem hard. With a little training, I'll be able to slay dragons and rescue damsels as well as any boy in Knight School."

"Ahhh, but there's a lot more to being a knight than riding off on exciting adventures," King Alexander told her. "It takes great honor, kindness, and sacrifice."

Princess Pulverizer didn't know how to respond to that one. Even she knew that honor, kindness, and sacrifice weren't exactly her strong points.

Things were not going Princess Pulverizer's way. Not at all.

That didn't happen often. But when it did, the princess knew exactly how to change her father's mind. All she had to do was give him her special face. It always made him smile. And laugh. *And do exactly what she wanted him to do.*

So Princess Pulverizer cocked her head to the side. She shot her father a broad, lopsided smile. Then she crossed her eyes.

A grin shot across King Alexander's face.

It was working!

The princess smiled a little wider. She crossed her eyes a little harder.

The king looked at his daughter's goofy smile and stared into her crossed eyes.

Finally, he said, "I suppose there's no real reason you can't go to Knight School . . ."

Yes! Princess Pulverizer pumped her fist in the air. The special face had done it again. Princess Pulverizer had gotten what she wanted.

". . . *eventually*," King Alexander continued. "But not today. Or even tomorrow."

Wait. What?

Princess Pulverizer dropped her fist and stared at her father. "I don't understand," she said.

"You have a lot to learn about what being a knight really means," King Alexander explained. "You have to *earn* your way into Knight School."

Princess Pulverizer scowled. This was not the answer she'd been hoping for.

"How am I supposed to do that?" she asked King Alexander.

"You must go on a Quest of Kindness," the king replied.

"A what?" Princess Pulverizer asked.

"A Quest of Kindness," King Alexander repeated. "I'm sending you out into the world. You must show bravery and do nice, unselfish acts for others. Only after you have completed eight good deeds will I allow you to enter Knight School."

"Eight?" Princess Pulverizer asked, her voice scaling up nervously. "That's an awful lot. Where will I find eight people who need my help in Empiria? I mean, we're a pretty small kingdom."

"You do not have to stay in Empiria," her father told her. "But I do not want you wandering too far, either. The world is a very big place. So for your own safety, you may only go as far as the mountains to the east and the river to the west. You may travel as far as the ocean to the south, and to the canyon to the north. That way you are always near enough to Empiria so my knights can search for you and save you if I find you are gone for a very long time."

"I won't need any saving," Princess Pulverizer assured him.

"Let's hope not," her father replied. "So we have a deal, then? You will go on a Quest of Kindness?"

The quest doesn't sound too awful, Princess Pulverizer thought. After all, she already did lots of good deeds for others. Didn't she always share her brussels sprouts with the royal dogs when the chef wasn't looking?

Although that probably wouldn't count as an actual good deed, because the dogs hated brussels sprouts as much as she did.

Still, there was also that one time when the princess had helped . . .

Or the day when she . . .

And how about . . .

Maybe this wasn't going to be so easy after all.

Unless . . .

Suddenly Princess Pulverizer got a great idea. What if she just went out into the world and wandered around for a few days? Then when she came back, she could just *tell* her father she had done eight good deeds.

She didn't actually have to *do* them.

"Okay, Papa," Princess Pulverizer said with a sly smile. "I will go on the quest."

"Wonderful," King Alexander said. "Oh, and one more thing. I will need you to bring back proof of each of your eight good deeds."

Princess Pulverizer frowned. How did her father always know what she was planning?

"How am I supposed to get proof?" Princess Pulverizer asked.

"I'm sure you'll figure it out," King Alexander replied. "After all, knights have to be smart, as well as brave and kind."

"But . . . ," Princess Pulverizer began to argue.

"You want to join the Knights of the Skround Table someday, right?" King Alexander asked her.

"Oh yes, Papa," Princess Pulverizer said. "More than anything."

"Well, then you'd better get going," the king said as he kissed his daughter on the forehead. "Your Quest of Kindness begins right now!"

CHAPTER 3

"Here, let me help you carry that heavy basket," Princess Pulverizer said the next morning as she came upon an old woman carrying a basket filled with potatoes.

The princess grinned widely as she spoke. She was just beginning her quest and hadn't gotten any farther than a small village on the outskirts of Empiria. Yet already she had found someone who appeared to need her help. What luck!

Princess Pulverizer tried to take the basket from the old woman's hands. But the woman wouldn't let go.

"Get your hands off my basket!" she demanded.

"But you *have* to let me help you," Princess Pulverizer insisted. She pulled harder at the basket.

"Let go of my potatoes!" The old woman gripped the basket tightly.

"I need to do a good deed," Princess Pulverizer explained. She gave another tug and . . .

Rrrippp. The basket broke open.

Thump.

Bump.

Flump.

The potatoes fell into the mud.

"Look what you've done!" the old woman scolded her. "My basket is torn. How am I supposed to get my potatoes home now?"

"I'll help you carry them," Princess Pulverizer suggested. "That would be a good deed, right?"

"I think you've done enough," the old woman said. "Go on your way."

"Can I at least take one of these potatoes as a token—just to show my father that I *tried* to do a good deed?" Princess Pulverizer asked.

"First you break my basket and now you want to steal one of my potatoes?" The woman gasped.

"I don't want to steal it, I just—" Princess Pulverizer began to explain.

But the old woman didn't let her finish. "HELP!" she shouted. "THIEF!"

A crowd of people turned and stared.

Uh-oh. Any minute now the sheriff would be there.

Princess Pulverizer could stay and try to explain to him that she was a princess on a Quest of Kindness so she could go to Knight School.

But considering no other girl had ever

gone on a quest like this, or gone to Knight School, she figured no sheriff in his right mind would ever believe her.

To him, she would just seem like a common thief—especially dressed as she was in a plain cloth tunic and cloak, carrying nothing but a simple knapsack.

Oh why hadn't she at least packed her royal tiara?

If she stuck around, Princess Pulverizer could be in big trouble. Maybe even wind up in the local dungeon!

So the princess did the only thing she could.

She ran off. As fast as possible.

Princess Pulverizer trudged her way up the hill. It seemed like she'd been running for hours. She was very tired. But at least now she was in another village—far from the old lady and her potatoes. She was safe.

Unfortunately, nearly a whole day had gone by and she still hadn't found a single person who needed her help. At this rate, her Quest for Kindness could go on forever.

The princess knelt down by a nearby stream and took a drink of cool, clear water. As she drank, two women came strolling down the path.

"The queen was absolutely beside herself," remarked the taller woman, who wore a pale green dress. "Some of the stolen jewels were gifts from her parents and her grandparents. They were priceless."

"I don't blame her for being upset," replied her friend. "The velvet, gem-covered box that held the jewels was stolen right out of her room while she was sleeping."

"I don't understand how that could happen," the woman in the green dress said. "The queen's chambers are in the top tower of the palace. She locks her door when she goes to sleep. The only way into her room is through the window."

"That tower is way too high for any ladder," the woman in the gray cloak added. "The thief would have had to be tall enough to actually reach in through the window and grab the jewels."

Her friend laughed. "That's not possible," she said. "No one in the entire kingdom of Shmergermeister is that tall."

"I doubt the queen will ever see her jewels again," the woman in the gray cloak said. "Who would be smart enough to know where to find someone that tall? Or brave enough to get the jewels back from such a thief?"

A smile began to form on Princess Pulverizer's face. *She* was smart. And *she* was brave. This was it! Her first task on her Quest of Kindness.

All she had to do was find someone tall enough to reach into a high tower window, retrieve the jewels, and return them to the queen.

Easy peasy.

Well, it would be—if she could figure out who the tallest person in the kingdom of Shmergermeister might be.

The princess remembered once reading a story about a tall, scary ogre who lived in an old, abandoned castle far up in the hills of a faraway kingdom. The ogre captured princesses and stole jewelry.

Hmmm . . . Princess Pulverizer was in a faraway kingdom. Okay, not *so* faraway. But there *were* hills all around her.

Sure, the ogre was just a character in a storybook. But storybook characters had to come from somewhere. Maybe there really was such a thing as a giant, jewel-stealing ogre.

Princess Pulverizer leaped to her feet and began searching the hills of

Shmergermeister for an ogre. It was no easy task. The roads were steep, and the ground was muddy. The tall, leafy trees made the forest seem dark and gloomy. But Princess Pulverizer kept walking, searching for a giant ogre.

Unfortunately, an hour later she still hadn't found a single sign of one.

This really stinks. Another dead end on my Quest of Kindness.

Just as she was about to turn back, Princess Pulverizer spotted something on the ground. It was a footprint.

A *giant* footprint.

A footprint so large and so wide, you could fit a family of five inside of it and still have room for a dog!

Up ahead, she saw another giant footprint.

And another.

And another.

Princess Pulverizer followed the giant footsteps up a steep, steep hill, until finally they led her to the largest castle she had ever seen.

It was also the *ugliest* castle she had ever seen. The wooden windowsills were rotting and lopsided. There were weeds growing all around. It looked like the place hadn't been cleaned in a hundred years. It was the perfect home for an ogre!

Quietly, Princess Pulverizer moved closer to the decrepit castle, making sure to stay hidden in the trees.

Suddenly, a loud, deep voice echoed through the hills. "SHINY!"

The princess jumped back. *Whoa!* That was scary.

But Princess Pulverizer was brave. Or at least she was trying to be.

I'm not afraid, she thought. *I'm not afraid*.

"SO SHINY!" the deep voice boomed, even louder this time.

Princess Pulverizer's knees knocked nervously. Her teeth began to chatter.

Okay, maybe she was a *little* afraid. But that wasn't going to stop her. She kept walking toward the castle. She moved closer. And closer. And closer still.

That's when she saw him.
The ogre. He looked just like the one in
her storybook.

The ogre was big.

And scary.

And really, really hairy! Boy, did he need a haircut.

The ogre was playing with some shiny gemstones. High atop his big, hairy head, he wore a teeny tiny crown. Well, it looked teeny tiny on the ogre, anyway. In reality, it was a crown that would fit perfectly on the head of a queen.

She had found them! The queen's jewels!

Now all she had to do was get them away from the ogre so she could return them to the Queen of Shmergermeister.

GRUMBLE. RUMBLE.

Suddenly, the loudest thunder the princess had ever heard echoed through the forest. But the sun was shining. And there wasn't a cloud in the sky.

How strange.

GRUMBLE. RUMBLE.

The ogre rubbed his belly. "ME HUNGRY," he grunted.

Now Princess Pulverizer understood. The thunder hadn't been coming from the sky at all. It was coming from deep inside the ogre's empty belly. It was time for his supper.

The ogre stood up and headed into his castle. The giant door shut behind him, and there was a click as the lock was turned.

Now the jewels were in the castle. Which meant Princess Pulverizer needed to go in there and get them.

But how? It wasn't like ogres just invited knights-in-training into their castles.

Or did they?

CHAPTER 4

"I am a happy princess wandering in the woods," Princess Pulverizer sang out as loudly as she could. *"All alone, with no one to protect me . . ."* The princess's voice cracked on that last note. She probably should have paid more attention to her music classes at the Royal School of Ladylike Manners.

Princess Pulverizer stopped singing and waited for the ogre to come capture her.

But the door to the castle didn't open.

Still, she wasn't giving up. She was going to get captured by that ogre, no matter how much singing she had to do. Being captured meant she would be brought inside the ogre's castle. And once she was in there, she could get her hands on the Queen of Shmergermeister's jewels.

"I'm all alone," Princess Pulverizer sang, much louder this time. *"Just picking flowers. With no one watching over me. And did I mention, I'm a princess?"*

She waited for a moment and stared at the door. It still didn't open.

What was wrong with this ogre? Didn't he know it was his job to capture princesses and drag them into his castle?

"La la la la!" Princess Pulverizer sang, so loud and so out of tune that it sounded more like squawking than singing.

Click. A lock opened. The door to the castle swung open. The ogre stomped out—with his dirty fingers shoved into his hairy ears.

"NOISE BAD," he grunted.

Princess Pulverizer scowled. "Come on. My singing's not *that* bad."

"BAD!" the ogre grumbled. "*VERY* BAD."

"Well, if my singing hurts your ears," Princess Pulverizer said angrily, "I'll just keep my mouth shut, then."

"FINE," the ogre bellowed. He turned and started back into his castle.

"Don't you want to capture me and hold me prisoner in your tower?" Princess Pulverizer asked him.

The ogre looked at her strangely. "NO SING?" he asked her.

The princess shook her head. "No more singing."

"OKAY," the ogre said. He took her by the arm and began dragging her inside. "I CAPTURE."

Princess Pulverizer sighed. It was about time.

◆ ◆ ◆ ◆ ◆

"YOU PRISONER," the ogre said as he led Princess Pulverizer up the last and steepest staircase and into the giant tower.

The princess could not believe her eyes. What a dump!

There were strange objects piled in a mound from floor to ceiling. Bent forks. Crusty spoons. Dulled metal knives. A broken hand mirror. Silk scarves. Copper teakettles. Frying pans. Broken teacups. Chipped dishes.

"What is all this junk?" Princess Pulverizer asked.

"TREASURES," the ogre barked at her. "*MY* TREASURES."

"Treasures?" the princess questioned. "This is just junk."

"MY TREASURES," the ogre repeated. "*YOU* NO TOUCH."

Princess Pulverizer looked at a large silver ladle that was covered in a crusty yellow film.

No touch.

No problem.

But a few minutes later, after the ogre had shut the tower door and left, Princess Pulverizer realized she just might have to dig through the pile of junk, after all.

The ogre had called this stuff *treasures*. So maybe the silverware, coins, pots, and pans were things he had stolen and wanted to keep for his own.

If so, it was possible that there were some *real* treasures in that mess.

Treasures from a jewelry box that was stolen from the Queen of Schmergermeister!

Princess Pulverizer had no choice. She reached into the pile of disgustingness and began to dig.

◆ ◆ ◆ ◆ ◆

After sorting through the ogre's treasures for what seemed like hours, Princess Pulverizer still had not found a single jewel.

The Queen of Schmergermeister's jewelry box was nowhere to be found.

But it had to be there in the castle. Princess Pulverizer had seen a queen's crown on the ogre's head. And she'd caught him playing with the gems.

Those jewels had to be somewhere else in the castle. But where?

ZZZZ . . . ZZZZZ . . . ZZZZ

A little while later, the castle suddenly began to rock.

And rumble.

And rattle all around.

ZZZZZ . . . ZZZ . . . ZZZZZZZ

Princess Pulverizer gulped. The ground was vibrating beneath her. It felt like any minute it would open up and swallow the castle whole.

ZZZZZZ . . . ZZZ

And what was that horrible noise? She'd never heard anything like it before.

Wait a minute. Yes, she had. That was the same sound Lady Frump had made one afternoon when the palace chef gave the girls a lecture on how to properly eat cucumber sandwiches.

The lesson had been so boring that even

Lady Frump had fallen asleep. And then she'd started snoring.

ZZZZ . . . ZZZ

That was it! The ogre had fallen asleep. His snoring was so loud, it was rocking the whole castle.

This was Princess Pulverizer's chance. All she had to do was find the jewels, grab them, and make her escape—before the ogre awoke.

How hard could that be?

Pretty hard, actually, if the ogre had locked the tower door behind him when he left.

Quickly, Princess Pulverizer raced to the door.

She jiggled the doorknob. And then . . .

The door popped open. Silly ogre. He'd forgotten to lock the princess in.

Lucky for her, the ogre seemed pretty new to this capturing-damsels thing.

As she quietly made her way down the stairs from the tower, Princess Pulverizer smiled smugly to herself. This Quest of Kindness was going to be a piece of cake.

ZZZZ ... ZZZZZ ...
ZZZZZZZZZZZZZZZ

The snoring grew louder and louder as the princess neared the ogre's chambers. Finally, she reached the room and snuck a peek through his open door.

The ogre was sleeping facedown on the floor, with his rear end high in the air like a giant ogre-butt mountain.

On the other side of the ogre-butt mountain was a beautiful velvet box encrusted with jewels.

That has to be the Queen of Shmergermeister's jewelry box, thought Princess Pulverizer. The ogre was keeping his newest, shiniest, nicest treasures close by.

Princess Pulverizer slid quickly and carefully around the sleeping ogre, making sure she stayed far from his humongous body.

When she reached the other side of him, Princess Pulverizer snatched the jewelry box. She shoved it into her knapsack and started back toward the door.

As she reached the doorway, the princess glanced over at the ogre one more time. That's when she noticed the sword beside him—probably another of his stolen treasures. Something like that might come in handy. Maybe she should just take it and . . .

ZZZZ . . . ZZZZZZZZZZZZZZZZZZ

Before the princess could grab the sword, the ogre let out the loudest snore she had ever heard.

And then he began to roll over . . .

"Yikes!" Princess Pulverizer leaped out of the way just in time. A moment later, she would have been crushed under the weight of the giant ogre.

That was the *good* news.

The *bad* news was the ogre was now awake. And it's never a great idea to wake a sleeping ogre.

"NO ESCAPE!" the ogre grunted as he leaped to his giant feet and grabbed the princess with his massive fingers.

"BACK TO TOWER!"

And with that, the ogre threw Princess Pulverizer over his shoulder and carried her back to the tower at the top of his castle. He put her down in the room, slammed the door, and locked it behind him.

Clearly, he had learned his lesson.

The princess was trapped in the tower. Stuck in there with all the smelly, moldy junk. And she had no way out.

This was *not* part of her plan.

"LET ME OUT OF HERE!" Princess Pulverizer shouted. "LET ME OUT!"

CHAPTER 5

Grrr . . .

Princess Pulverizer was mad. *Really* mad. She couldn't believe she'd been stuck in the ogre's tower for a whole night.

Her plan had been going so well. She'd gotten into the castle with no problems. She'd found the queen's jewels—and stolen them back.

But here it was the next morning, and she was still stuck in the ogre's castle.

And it wasn't like anyone was going to be looking for her, or even missing her. No one—not even her own father—would be expecting her. Not for a long while. After all, performing eight good deeds took time.

It would be weeks—maybe months—until the Knights of the Skround Table would be sent to look for her.

Not that she really *needed* help. Because there *had* to be a way for her to get out. And if anybody could figure out how to escape, it was Princess Pulverizer.

The ogre was big. And strong. But he wasn't smart. And smart could always outsmart strong. That was why they called it out*smart*. All the princess had to do was *think* her way out of this mess.

Except it was really, really hard to think on an empty stomach! Boy, was she hungry.

THUMP. THUMP.

Suddenly, the whole castle began to shake.

THUMP. THUMP.

Princess Pulverizer gulped. It sounded like the ogre was walking up the stairs to the tower. What did he want now? Had he figured out that she'd stolen back the queen's jewels?

Princess Pulverizer sure hoped not. Because there was no telling what that big stupid lunk would do if he got angry.

Sniff . . . sniff . . . ewwwww.

As the ogre got closer, a terrible smell wafted up into the tower. It smelled like dirty feet and underarm sweat.

Princess Pulverizer frowned. That giant monster didn't just need a haircut. He needed a bath, too.

Click. A moment later, the ogre opened the door. He shoved a bowl and a spoon into the princess's hands.

"FOOD," he bellowed. Then he turned

and left the tower, locking the door behind him.

The smell of dirty feet and underarm sweat filled the tower. And it didn't leave with the ogre. That was because it wasn't the ogre that smelled so bad. It was the gruel he'd served her for breakfast!

The only good thing about a breakfast like this was that the princess didn't have to figure out which spoon was the proper one to use when eating gruel.

Because princesses did not eat gruel. *Ever.*

Still, she was hungry. And this was food. Sort of. So she took a spoonful, swished it around in her mouth, and . . .

Spit the nasty stuff across the room.

"THIS IS DISGUSTING!" she shouted. "I WANT EGGS, AND A ROLL, AND SOME COLD JUICE!"

The princess waited for a moment, expecting the ogre to hurry back up with a new breakfast—perhaps on a tray this time.

But Princess Pulverizer didn't hear any footsteps on the stairs.

Hmmm . . . Maybe the ogre hadn't heard her. If he had, he surely would have returned with a better meal.

"I AM A PRINCESS," she shouted, louder this time. "I DO NOT EAT SLOP! ARE YOU BRINGING ME MY BREAKFAST? ARE YOU OUT THERE? ANSWER ME!"

"Do not worry, damsel in distress!"

Surprisingly, the princess got an answer. Only it wasn't the answer to her question. And it wasn't coming from inside the castle.

It was coming from outside.

Princess Pulverizer hurried to the tower window and looked down. There was a young knight standing below.

"I will save you!" the knight called up to her in a squeaky, nervous voice.

Princess Pulverizer frowned. That little knight didn't look like he could save a mouse from a cat—never mind a princess from an ogre.

Luckily, the last thing Princess Pulverizer needed was saving. She could get out of this mess all on her own.

Besides, if this little knight got involved, he'd probably want to share the credit for returning the Queen of Shmergermeister's jewels. That was *not* happening. Not when Princess Pulverizer had already gone through so much to get the jewels back.

"Go away!" she called down to the little knight. "You're ruining everything."

"Don't worry!" the knight called back. "My faithful companion and I are here to free you and . . ."

That was the last thing Princess Pulverizer heard from the little knight, because at just that moment, the ogre rushed out of the castle. He scooped up the knight with one hand and threw him over his shoulder.

With the other hand, he reached out and grabbed some sort of creature by the tail. The princess didn't have time to get a good look at what kind of creature it was. All she knew was that it was bright green and nearly the size of a fat horse.

THUMP. THUMP.

The ogre was coming up the stairs again. By now the princess recognized his footsteps.

THUD. THUD. THUD. THUD.

Those weren't the ogre's footsteps. They were loud. And heavy. But they didn't belong to the ogre. They had to belong to the creature that had been captured along with the knight.

THUD. THUD. THUD. THUD. SOB!

The princess heard a loud, mournful roar. It sounded way too loud for any human to make.

Princess Pulverizer had no idea what kind of monster could make a loud, horrible noise like that. All she knew was she didn't want to meet him.

A moment later, the tower door opened. The ogre stomped in and . . . *CLANG.* He dropped the little knight right on his armor-covered rear end.

Then the ogre yanked at the creature's long, green, spiny tail and pulled him into the room.

Princess Pulverizer's eyes opened wide.
The creature was a dragon. A real, live
dragon!

"MY PRISONERS!" the ogre
bellowed as he left the tower
and headed back down
the stairs.

The loud crying
started up again
immediately.
Surprisingly, the loud
cries were coming
from a human.
The tiny knight
was sobbing
hysterically.

Wow! For a little guy, he sure could make a lot of noise.

BELCH!

Just then, the dragon let out a giant burp. A horrible smell filled the air. It stank even worse than the gruel.

"Sorry," the dragon apologized. "Sometimes when I eat too much, I get a little gassy. And I had a huge breakfast today."

Princess Pulverizer shook her head. She was stuck in a garbage-filled tiny tower with a gassy green dragon and a blubbering knight. And she had nothing to eat but gruel that smelled like feet and sweat.

This quest had become quite a mess.

CHAPTER 6

"It's getting a little crowded in here," Princess Pulverizer complained as she stared at her new companions. "And there's no way out, is there?" the knight said. *SOB. SOB.*

Princess Pulverizer gave him a threatening stare. "Don't start that again," she warned him.

The knight took a deep breath and choked back his cries. Then he bowed. "I am Lucas."

"Don't you mean *Sir* Lucas?" Princess Pulverizer asked him.

"Not exactly," Lucas told her. "I'm just a knight-in-training. Or I was, until I left Knight School."

Princess Pulverizer couldn't believe her ears. This Lucas kid had left Knight School! "Why would anybody leave Knight School?" she asked him. "Knight School is the greatest place on earth."

"I didn't leave it on purpose," Lucas told her. "I was kind of laughed out."

Princess Pulverizer stared at him. "Why?" she asked him.

Lucas turned bright red. "I just couldn't do anything right," he told her. "I left my armor out in the rain overnight. Now look at it."

The princess looked closely at Lucas's armor. It was covered with spots of rust.

"That's not the worst of it," Lucas continued. "One time I was practicing fencing with my partner, and the visor on my helmet slammed shut. I couldn't see a thing. But I kept fencing."

"That was very noble of you," Princess Pulverizer said.

"It was very *stupid* of me," Lucas corrected her. "I kept waving my sword around and around—and I had no idea that I was actually fencing with a tree branch, until it fell on my head."

Princess Pulverizer started to laugh. She stopped when she saw the expression on Lucas's face.

"It's okay," Lucas told her. "Go ahead and laugh. Everybody else did."

Princess Pulverizer smiled at him. "That really doesn't sound so bad," she said. "Certainly not bad enough to make you leave Knight School."

"Well, there's also one more thing," Lucas said. "But it's really embarrassing."

Princess Pulverizer stared at him. It would have to be pretty bad to be more embarrassing than fencing with a tree branch.

"You see, I'm a—" Lucas began. He stopped mid-sentence and leaped up onto a wooden stool. "MOUSE!" he shouted.

Princess Pulverizer looked down. Sure enough, a little gray mouse was scooting around on the floor.

"You're afraid of a mouse?" she asked Lucas.

He nodded. "I'm pretty much afraid of everything," Lucas

admitted. "The other guys nicknamed me Lucas the Lily-Livered. That really hurt my feelings. So I left."

"You left?" Princess Pulverizer asked him. "But where did you go? Where do you live now?"

"I don't have a home," Lucas said. "I've just been wandering the woods. For a while I was alone. Then I met Dribble. It's been good to have a friend."

"Dribble?" Princess Pulverizer asked. "What kind of a name is that for a dragon?"

"Well, what's *your* name?" Dribble asked her.

"Princess Pulverizer," she replied proudly.

"What kind of a name is that for a princess?" Dribble asked her.

"It's a great name for a princess," Princess Pulverizer insisted. "Especially for a princess who is going to go to Knight School."

"Knight School?" Lucas asked her. "But you can't go to Knight School!"

Princess Pulverizer put her hands on her hips. She stared angrily at Lucas. "And why not?" she demanded.

Lucas gulped. "Well . . . because . . . I mean . . . you're a . . . well . . . you're a princess."

"There's no rule that a princess can't be a knight," she told him. "My father, King Alexander of Empiria, has decreed that I can go to Knight School—after I do eight good deeds."

"Have you done any good deeds yet?" Lucas asked her.

"I was in the middle of doing one when you guys showed up," Princess Pulverizer told him. "I have retrieved the Queen of Shmergermeister's jewels from the evil ogre. And when I get out of here, I will return them to her."

"How do you plan to get out of here?" Lucas asked her.

"I don't know, exactly," Princess Pulverizer told him. "But I do know it would have been a lot easier for me to sneak out before you and your dragon showed up. Now the ogre is on his guard. He's going to be watching us all very carefully."

"We just wanted to rescue you," Dribble told her. He let out another belch. The powerful smelly wind knocked the princess to the ground.

But not even a dragon burp could keep Princess Pulverizer down. She scrambled to her feet and glared at him.

"I didn't need your help!" Princess

Pulverizer snapped at Dribble. "Why does everyone think girls need rescuing? I can get out of here by myself. And I can do eight good deeds all on my own. In fact . . ." A smile flashed across Princess Pulverizer's face. "Thanks to you, I'm going to get to do two good deeds today," she told Dribble.

"Thanks to *me*?" Dribble asked her.

"Yep," the princess said. "I'm going to steal that ogre's sword. And right before I leave the castle, I'm going to slay you."

Dribble stared at the princess with his huge dragon eyes. "Why would you want to do that to me?" he asked her.

"Because dragons are mean," Princess Pulverizer explained. "They breathe fire and burn villages. Think of all the people I will save if I slay a dragon."

"B-b-but," Dribble stammered. He seemed too shocked to answer her.

"You can't slay Dribble," Lucas told the princess. "He's my friend. He's not mean at all."

"Don't you breathe fire?" Princess Pulverizer asked him.

"Sure," Dribble told her. "But not to burn villages."

"Then what do you use your fire for?" Princess Pulverizer asked.

Lucas turned and smiled at Dribble.

"Show her," he said.

"She said she wanted to slay me," Dribble said sadly. A giant dragon-size tear spilled out of his eye.

"Show her," Lucas repeated.

Princess Pulverizer turned to Lucas. "You're asking a fire-breathing dragon to breathe fire— here? Are you nuts? He's gonna burn this place down. *With us in it!*"

"Wait and see," Lucas told her. "You're never going to believe what Dribble can do."

CHAPTER 7

"Grilled cheese?" Princess Pulverizer asked
with surprise a few minutes later. "You use
your fire-breathing ability to make *grilled
cheese?*"

Dribble nodded and let out another
blast of fire. He gently turned the
sandwich with his foot to make sure it was
evenly toasted on both sides.

"Not just grilled cheese," Lucas corrected her. "The greatest grilled cheese sandwiches you will ever taste in any kingdom. He's an amazing chef."

"I've never heard of a dragon who was a chef before," Princess Pulverizer said.

"I've never heard of a princess who wanted to go to Knight School before," Dribble replied.

Princess Pulverizer scowled. He had her there.

"Try a sandwich," Lucas told her.

"How do I know this evil dragon didn't poison it?" Princess Pulverizer asked.

Dribble looked at her sadly. "I'm not evil." He let some wind out from under his tail—and a terrible smell filled the air. "Excuse me," he apologized. "I'm gassy. But I'm not evil," he insisted.

"Dribble wouldn't poison anyone," Lucas assured Princess Pulverizer.

"You take a bite first," the princess ordered Lucas. "Be my royal taster."

"If you say so," Lucas said with a shrug. He broke off a piece of the sandwich and popped it into his mouth. "Mmmm . . . Limburger cheese. My favorite."

"Limburger is so smelly," Princess Pulverizer complained. "Why not cheddar?"

"Because limburger cheese is what I have in my knapsack," Lucas said. "Try it. You'll like it."

Princess Pulverizer wasn't so sure. But she was hungry. And grilled cheese was definitely a step up from gruel.

So the princess took a bite.

"Mmmm . . . ," she said. "This is delicious."

"I told you so," Dribble said. "I'm going to be a chef one day."

"The other dragons in your lair are lucky to have you," Princess Pulverizer told him.

Another giant tear slid down Dribble's face.

"What did I say now?" Princess Pulverizer demanded.

"It's just that the other dragons don't want Dribble in their lair," Lucas explained. "They don't think dragons should use their fire-breathing for good. So they kicked him out."

Princess Pulverizer looked at Lucas and Dribble. "You two are a real pair of misfits, aren't you?" she said.

"What about you?" Dribble asked.

"What *about* me?" she countered.

"Were you wandering around with a bunch of other princesses when you were captured?" Dribble asked her.

"No," she replied. "I'm doing this quest all on my own."

"So, basically, you don't fit in, either," Dribble suggested.

Hmmm . . . He has a point.

Princess Pulverizer took another bite of her sandwich. "This tastes really great, Dribble," she said. "Even if it does smell stinky."

"Stinky cheese is the best," Lucas told her. "The stinkier the better."

Suddenly, the ogre's grunts rang through the castle. "SOMETHING SMELLY!"

"I don't know what he's complaining about," Princess Pulverizer said. "Has he smelled his pits lately?"

"NO LIKE SMELLY!" the ogre bellowed.

STOMP. STOMP. STOMP. STOMP.

"Uh-oh!" Lucas cried out. "He's on his way up here." *Sob! Sob!*

"No more crying!" the princess warned him angrily.

"B-b-but the ogre sounds really angry," Lucas said. "He might hurt us. *Or worse.*"

"Don't worry," Princess Pulverizer told them. "That ogre won't get near us!"

"Who's going to stop him?" Dribble asked her.

Princess Pulverizer looked from the lily-livered knight-in-training to the gassy, not-at-all-scary dragon. They weren't going to be much help.

"Who else?" she asked them. "Me. The mighty Princess Pulverizer!"

CHAPTER 8

THUMP. THUMP. The ogre's footsteps were closer now. Princess Pulverizer needed a plan.

What would a knight do in a case like this?

He would probably use his sword and stab the ogre in the chest. But the princess didn't

have a sword. All she had was her brains, her arms, and her legs.

Whoosh! At just that moment, the door to the tower flew open. The ogre was standing there, glowering at his prisoners.

"SMELLY!" he bellowed. "STINKY . . ."

Slam!

Princess Pulverizer kicked the ogre in his knee—hard.

Bam! She kicked him in the other knee—even harder. And when the ogre bent down to grab his injured knees . . .

Wham! The princess grabbed a wooden chair and smashed the ogre right in the stomach.

The ogre tilted backward, grabbing his middle.

"OOO. OOO. OW!" He banged his head on the doorpost.

Princess Pulverizer leaped out of the way, and over to the far window near her friends, just before . . .

Thud! The ogre fell to the ground in a heap right in the middle of the room.

"Wow!" Lucas said. "I had no idea you were that strong."

"I'm not," Princess Pulverizer admitted. "I just caught him by surprise."

"Is he dead?" Lucas wondered nervously.

"Nah," Princess Pulverizer said. "I can still smell his awful breath. He's just knocked out. But he won't be for long. We have to get out of here."

"How are we going to do that?" Dribble asked her. "He's blocking the doorway."

"Maybe we could climb over him," Lucas suggested.

"He would feel us and wake up," Princess Pulverizer said. "Especially you, big guy," she added, pointing to Dribble.

"It's not my fault I'm big," Dribble told her. "That's how dragons are supposed to be."

"We're trapped!" Lucas cried out.

"Don't worry, I'll think of something," Princess Pulverizer said. "I always do. I thought of a way to get myself into the castle, didn't I?"

"I wish you had thought of a way *out*," Dribble muttered under his dragon breath. He stared longingly out the window. "We're going to be stuck in here forever. I'm never going to feel the grass under my feet again. And I'm never going to get to open my own restaurant."

Sob. Lucas began to cry again.

The princess covered her ears. It was hard to think with the sound of crying.

BURP! Dribble let out another loud belch. The powerful wind was so strong, it shook the ogre's giant mountain of stolen treasures.

Princess Pulverizer was absolutely miserable. Being stuck in a tower with a gassy dragon was really the worst.

She'd never met anyone who let out so much smelly air.

Or who cried as much as Lucas did.

How on earth was she going to get them all out of this mess?

She looked over at Dribble. He was batting his wings up and down, trying to get rid of the smell from his latest belch.

A broad smile formed on Princess Pulverizer's face.

"That's it!" she shouted excitedly. "Dribble is going to save us all!"

CHAPTER 9

"Wait—what?" Dribble asked. "*I'm* going to save us?"

"You sure are," Princess Pulverizer assured him.

Dribble grinned his approval. "I like helping people," he said happily. "Just tell me what I have to do!"

"UGGGHHHH!" Just then, the ogre let out a loud groan. He rolled onto his side.

"He's waking up," Lucas sobbed. "He's

going to be so mad. He'll lock us in here and throw away the key."

"Quick!" Princess Pulverizer ordered Lucas. "Climb onto Dribble's back."

"Why should I do that?" Lucas asked her.

"Yes, why should he do that?" Dribble asked.

"Because you're going to fly us right out this window," Princess Pulverizer told the dragon. "That's my plan."

"F-f-fly?" Lucas asked nervously. "Like in the air?"

"Don't worry, Lucas," Dribble said.

"Why? Because you're such a great flyer?" Princess Pulverizer wondered excitedly.

"No," Dribble said. "Because I can't fly. I still have my baby wings. My adult wings haven't grown in yet. Baby wings aren't big or strong enough to fly."

Princess Pulverizer frowned. "You're not a full-grown dragon?" she asked. "But you're huge."

"Not for a dragon," Dribble told her. "Grown-up dragons are humongous. I'm sorry," he apologized. He looked longingly back out the window. And let out another giant burp. "Boy, does my stomach hurt. I should never have had that third grilled cheese sandwich this morning."

Dribble's burp was so powerful, it blew some of the ogre's treasures off the top of the mountain.

Princess Pulverizer watched from her spot near the window as a shiny soup pot, carving knife, and teakettle tumbled over the ogre's giant body, out the door, and right down the stairs.

"That's it!" Princess Pulverizer shouted excitedly.

"What's it?" Dribble and Lucas asked at the same time.

"I've got a new plan," she told them. "A *better* plan."

"Yay!" Dribble shouted. Lucas stopped

crying immediately.

"HEAD HURT!" At just that moment, the ogre began to stir again. "OWIE!"

"He's waking up!" Lucas cried out.

Burp.

Dribble let out a belch. It wasn't a big burp by dragon standards. But it was strong enough to blow a frying pan off the top of the garbage mountain. The pan fell and bonked the ogre on the head.

"NIGHTY NIGHT," the ogre groaned as he passed out again.

"He's not going to stay that way for long,"

Dribble told Princess Pulverizer. "If you've got a plan, now's a good time to put it into motion."

"Okay," Princess Pulverizer told the dragon. "But first, you probably should have a little snack."

Dribble looked at the princess like she was crazy. "You want me to eat now?"

"I don't think this is a good time for food," Lucas said.

"It's the perfect time," Princess Pulverizer insisted. She held up the bowl of old gruel. "Come on, Dribble. Just a little spoonful."

"I'm not hungry," Dribble protested. "And besides, that stuff smells disgusting."

Princess Pulverizer frowned. This was not going the way she had hoped.

"Please, Dribble, open wide," the princess urged as she held the spoonful of vile stuff up to his mouth. "Here comes the chariot, bringing food to your tummy. Take a bite. Yummy yum yummy . . ."

Before Dribble even realized what was happening, Princess Pulverizer shoved a heaping spoonful of gooey gruel into his mouth.

"What is that stuff?" Dribble asked, gagging.

"It's the stuff that's going to save us," Princess Pulverizer told him, shoving another heaping spoonful into Dribble's mouth. "Over the teeth and over the gums—look out, stomach, here it comes."

Dribble swallowed the pasty, smelly, cold gruel and made a face. "What is wrong with you?" he asked. "Doesn't my stomach already hurt enough? One more spoonful of that stuff and I think I might explode."

"That's exactly what I'm counting on," Princess Pulverizer said as she shoved the last nasty spoonful of gruel right down his throat.

Princess Pulverizer smiled excitedly as Dribble let out a massive belch. She figured it had to be the loudest, windiest, smelliest burp in the history of the world.

And it was exactly what they needed.

CRASH!

CLANK!

CLUNK!

KERPLUNK!

The sheer force of Dribble's giant burp suddenly toppled the ogre's pile of treasures!

Cups, bottles, silverware, teakettles, and other shiny stuff began raining down and buried the evil ogre.

Then it began cascading down the stairs in a giant avalanche of junk.

"WHAT HAPPENING?!" the angry ogre shouted from beneath the giant pile of his precious stolen treasure.

"Come on, you guys!" Princess Pulverizer ordered. "We're getting out of here."

"How?" Dribble asked her.

"We're going sledding," Princess Pulverizer said.

Dribble gave her a funny look. "How are we going to sled? There's no snow in here."

Princess Pulverizer shook her head. "We don't need snow," she told him. "We're going to slide right over the ogre, down this moving mountain of junk, and out the front door."

"I don't like sledding," Lucas said. "You can get hurt. One time I sledded right into a fence and I . . ."

Princess Pulverizer did not have time to

listen to Lucas's story. She had to get him moving.

So she pushed him headfirst down the avalanche of junk.

"AAHHHH!" Lucas cried as he bumped and thumped his way over the ogre and down the stairs on his stomach.

"Your turn, Dribble," Princess Pulverizer said. "Hurry."

Dribble didn't need a push—which was good, since he was *way* too heavy for Princess Pulverizer to push, anyway. The dragon just plopped down on his big green bottom and slid down the stairs along with the gushing river of garbage.

Then it was Princess Pulverizer's turn.

"Hey, you guys!" she called as she slid her way to freedom. "Look out below!"

CHAPTER 11

A few seconds later, the princess, the knight, and the dragon were all safely outside the ogre's castle. But Princess Pulverizer knew it wouldn't be long before the ogre dug his way out of the pile of what was left of his treasures. And when he did, he was sure to come after them.

"Okay, Dribble," she said. "The only thing left for you to do now is carry us to safety."

"Why do I have to carry you guys?" Dribble asked her. "You can run all on your own."

"Yes, we can," Princess Pulverizer agreed. "But Lucas and I only have two feet each. You have four. You can move faster."

Dribble thought about that for a moment. He was obviously unable to come up with an argument, because he finally said, "Okay, climb on."

Lucas scrambled onto his friend's back. He climbed up high on Dribble's neck. "Please don't let me fall off," he begged.

"Don't worry, pal," Dribble assured him. "I would never let anything happen to you."

Princess Pulverizer climbed up the dragon's tail and onto his back. "Okay, Dribble!" she ordered. "Take us to the Queen of Shmergermeister!"

It seemed to Princess Pulverizer that she and Lucas had been riding on Dribble's back for a very long time. She was tired. And hungry. And very, very cranky.

To make matters worse, Dribble was still feeling pretty gassy. So not only was the ride bumpy, it was smelly, too.

"I sure could go for one of those grilled cheese sandwiches now," Princess Pulverizer grumbled. "I'm starving."

"Don't complain," Dribble called back to her between huffs and puffs. "I'm the one doing all the work here. This is the longest road I've ever been on. Are you sure we're going in the right direction?"

"The two women were definitely heading this way when I heard them talking about the queen's jewels," Princess Pulverizer told him. "And they were definitely from Shmergermeister."

"I see a palace!" Lucas shouted out suddenly from his perch high atop Dribble's neck. "It's just up that big hill."

"I can't climb another hill," Dribble groaned.

"Sure you can," Princess Pulverizer said.

"No, I can't," Dribble insisted. "My stomach hurts too badly. Probably because *someone* fed me way too much gruel."

Princess Pulverizer frowned. Maybe she had gone a *little* too far with that last spoonful.

"How about we take a break?" she suggested finally. "Dribble, you need the rest. And we could all use a little snack."

"Not me," Dribble groaned as he let out another stinky burp. "I don't want to see food again for a long time."

"Come on, just one little sandwich," the princess pleaded. She cocked her head to one side, smiled broadly, and crossed her eyes.

"Are you okay?" Dribble asked her. "You look kind of ill."

Princess Pulverizer frowned. Apparently, her special face had no effect on dragons.

"I'm kind of hungry, too. If you wouldn't mind making a few little sandwiches, I'd really appreciate it, Dribble," Lucas asked politely.

"Okay, pal, sure," Dribble said. "Since you asked so nicely."

Princess Pulverizer was amazed. All Lucas had to do to get what he wanted was ask politely. Wow.

Who would have thought *that* would work?

"Mmmm . . . ," Princess Pulverizer said a little while later as she took a big bite of her grilled cheese sandwich. "This tastes amazing."

"Dribble's the best dragon chef anywhere," Lucas said proudly.

Princess Pulverizer laughed. "He's probably the *only* dragon chef anywhere," she said.

Dribble gave her a look.

Princess Pulverizer frowned. The dragon sure was sensitive.

"But that doesn't mean your grilled cheese isn't delicious," she added quickly.

"Thank you," Dribble replied.

"Lucas, we're really lucky you brought cheese and bread with you," Princess Pulverizer continued. "That was good thinking. We all might have starved otherwise."

"I guess Lucas and I are kind of handy to have around," Dribble said to the princess.

Princess Pulverizer looked at the dragon, who had burped her to safety. Then she looked at the timid knight-in-training, who had come prepared with food.

The princess hated to admit it, but Dribble was right. "I guess I do need a little help sometimes," she said.

Dribble smiled. "The three of us actually make a pretty good team," he said.

"Team?" Princess Pulverizer asked. "Who said anything about a team? I'm on this Quest of Kindness on my own."

"You'll never get into Knight School that way," Lucas told her.

"Why not?" the princess demanded.

"Because knights are all about teamwork. They taught us that when I was in Knight School. You have to learn to work well with others," Lucas said.

Hmmm . . . Princess Pulverizer thought about that for a moment. The Royal Knights of Empiria did seem to go off on their quests in groups.

Maybe that was because they each had their own talents—and their own failings. Each knight picked up the others' slack.

"Well, come on, then," Princess Pulverizer said as she suddenly hopped to her feet.

"Come on where?" Dribble asked her.

"To the Shmergermeister castle," the princess replied. "I . . . er . . . I mean, *we* have some jewels to return!"

CHAPTER 12

"My jewels!" the Queen of
Shmergermeister exclaimed as Princess
Pulverizer handed her the velvet box.
"Wherever did you find them?"

"In an ogre's castle," Princess Pulverizer replied. "I got myself captured so I could retrieve them for you."

"You got yourself captured on purpose?" The queen sounded very surprised.

Princess Pulverizer nodded. "It was the only way. Dribble and Lucas got *themselves* captured, too. Good thing, because it took all three of us to get out of there."

"That was very brave," the queen said.

Princess Pulverizer looked over at her friends. She wasn't completely sure, but she thought Lucas was standing a little taller all of a sudden.

The Queen of Shmergermeister opened the velvet box and pulled out a large ruby ring. "This is a reward for your bravery," she said, handing the ring to Princess Pulverizer.

"Thank you," Princess Pulverizer replied. "But I'm trying to be a knight. And knights don't wear rings."

"They would if they knew about the ring's special powers," the queen said.

Special powers? Suddenly, the princess was very interested in the ruby ring. "What special powers?" she asked.

"The person who wears this ring is able to walk with complete silence," the queen said. "Not even a dry leaf will crackle under her feet."

"How would that be helpful?" Dribble asked.

"Are you kidding?" Princess Pulverizer replied. "This ring will let us sneak up on our enemies. It gives us the element of surprise."

"W-w-we have en-en-enemies?" Lucas stammered.

"Sure," Princess Pulverizer told him. "All knights have enemies."

Lucas frowned nervously.

"I suspect you will be able to defeat them," the queen assured him. "You three are very powerful together."

"The power of three." Princess Pulverizer smiled. "I like that."

"Now, please take this ring as a token of my gratitude," the Queen of Shmergermeister told Princess Pulverizer. "I insist."

Princess Pulverizer took the ruby ring and slipped it onto her finger. It was a perfect fit.

The ring was a really lovely gift. And better still, it was proof that she had completed her first task in her Quest of Kindness.

But there were seven more such tasks to go. So . . .

"We must be taking our leave," Princess Pulverizer said with a curtsy.

"Hey, you do that really well," Dribble complimented her.

"I've had a lot of practice," Princess Pulverizer told him. "Lady Frump made us do one hundred curtsies every day. I guess it came in handy after all."

"Can't we stay awhile longer?" Lucas pleaded. "There are so many scary things out there in the world. I feel safer inside this castle."

"You may stay as long as you like," the queen told him.

But Princess Pulverizer wasn't staying put. There was too much to do.

"Come on, you two," she said to Lucas and Dribble. "We have to go. There are a lot of people out there who need help. And we are just the ones to help them!"

THE QUEST
CONTINUES . . .

and NOW, HeRe's a
sneak peek at the Next

PRiNceSS
PULVeRiZeR

worse, worser, wurst

"AAAAAHHH! There's a MONSTER
in that tree!" Lucas cried out. "A hairy,
creepy-crawly MONSTER!"

The scared knight-in-training dropped
the grilled cheese sandwich he'd been
snacking on and ran off as fast as he could.

"A *monster*?" Princess Pulverizer repeated.
But she did not sound scared at all.

Nothing scared Princess Pulverizer.

Well, *very little* scared her, anyway.

"Y-y-yes," Lucas answered from his favorite hiding spot—crouched behind his best friend, Dribble the dragon. "I hate things that creep and crawl!"

"I'll defeat it!" Princess Pulverizer said, leaping to her feet.

"H-h-how?" Lucas stammered nervously. "You don't have any weapons."

"Sure I do." The princess bent her arms to show off her muscles. "These!"

Lucas and Dribble did not seem particularly impressed.

But that wasn't stopping Princess Pulverizer. "*Watch out, monster! You are no match for me,*" she shouted.

Princess Pulverizer looked up into the tree. But she didn't see a monster. She didn't see anything other than the usual branches, leaves, and blossoms.

Hmmm . . . Maybe the monster was hiding.

The princess leaped into the air and grabbed a tree branch. She pulled herself up and began climbing, searching for a monster hidden in the leaves.

But there was no monster anywhere.

Suddenly, out of the corner of her eye, Princess Pulverizer noticed a black, white, and yellow hairy creature creeping and crawling on a branch.

Wait a minute.

Hairy?

Creeping?

Crawling?

Oh brother. Lucas hadn't seen a monster at all. He'd seen a *caterpillar.*

Princess Pulverizer wasn't surprised that

Lucas was afraid of an insect. Lucas was afraid of *everything*.

The princess let the little caterpillar crawl onto her finger. She tucked him in her pocket and slid down to the ground.

Princess Pulverizer walked over to her friends and dangled the tiny creature in front of Lucas's nose. "Is this your monster?"

Lucas shuddered. "Get that away from me!" he cried out.

Princess Pulverizer laughed.

Dribble looked from the caterpillar to Lucas and back again. He clenched his dragon lips together tightly, trying not to laugh. But he couldn't help himself.

"Ha-ha-ha-ha . . ." *SNORT!* Dribble laughed so hard, the ground shook beneath him.

"This isn't a monster," Princess Pulverizer told Lucas. "It's a caterpillar." She placed the stunned insect back on a low-hanging tree branch.

Lucas turned red with embarrassment. "I really hate things that creep and crawl," he said timidly.

"Aaaachoooo!" Suddenly, Dribble let out a loud, powerful sneeze.

"Gesundheit," Lucas said. "Are you getting a cold?"

The dragon shook his head. "It's those apple blossoms. I'm allergic. Aaachoooo!"

That last sneeze was so strong, it blew Lucas over. He fell backward onto the ground.

"Sorry," Dribble apologized as Lucas scrambled back to his feet.

"It's okay," Lucas assured him.

The dragon looked down at the two grilled cheese sandwiches his friends had dropped. "What a waste of cheese," he said. "It's too bad you guys didn't finish them. Gouda grilled cheese is my specialty."

"I'm sorry," Lucas apologized. "But it's not a total waste. The ants seem to be enjoying them."

"I'm sorry, too," Princess Pulverizer grumbled. "I'm sorry I couldn't save you from a creepy-crawly, hairy monster. Because that would have been a good deed."

"A very good deed *in*deed," Lucas agreed.

to be continued . . .

Nancy Krulik

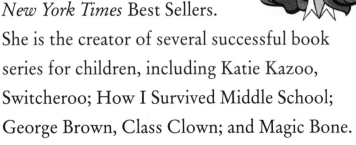

is the author of more than two hundred books for children and young adults, including three *New York Times* Best Sellers. She is the creator of several successful book series for children, including Katie Kazoo, Switcheroo; How I Survived Middle School; George Brown, Class Clown; and Magic Bone. Visit Nancy at realnancykrulik.com.

Ben Balistreri

has been working for more than twenty years in the animation industry. He's won an Emmy Award for his character designs and has been nominated for nine Annie Awards, winning once. His art can be seen in *Tangled: The Series*, *How to Train Your Dragon*, and many more.